M.L. Buchman is guaranteed to get me lost in a good story.

I love Buchman's writing. His vivid descriptions bring everything to life in an unforgettable way.

CROSSING THE BAR

A US COAST GUARD ROMANCE

M. L. BUCHMAN

Buchman Bookworks

Other works by M. L. Buchman:

"This is Carlos Torres and you're listening to *Crossing the Bar* where I bring you the latest news of what ships are crossing the Columbia River Bar. Today I also have on the radio the newest Surfman of the US Coast Guard search-and-rescue team stationed nearby at Cape D, that's Cape Disappointment, Washington. Actually, she's the newest Surf*woman*. But first, here's what ships are crossing the bar today."

Carlos sat in the small, circular tower that had always been the home of *Crossing the Bar*. His aunt had started it as a lark when she was between jobs, doing what she could to learn more about the ships she could watch entering the Columbia River from the window of her Astoria, Oregon late-Victorian home. Her podcast became an overnight phenomenon. At her listeners' request, she began learning what the ships were carrying in their holds. She then added in their last port of call, their owners, and even tidbits of their history—like just how many different flags they'd sailed under.

When she added interviews her podcast had changed from a local success to become the second most popular shipping news show anywhere in the world, coming in second only to the BBC's historic 150-year-old *Shipping Forecast*.

For months she'd been teasing him about taking over the show before she "withered at the microphone." As if. Women like Aunt Roz lived forever—at least he hoped so. When he'd finally confessed to a little interest—she'd instantly flown to Japan and booked a three-week passage on a car carrier running a load of Subarus from Japan back to Portland, Oregon, her idea of a fun vacation—and left the show to him to try out.

If it *had* been his idea, he'd probably have called the show *The Graveyard of the Pacific*. Over two thousand wrecks littered the sea floor around the Columbia Bar—the massive undersea sandbars churning gigantic surf even on the quietest days. It was generally acknowledged as the most dangerous shipping waters in the world.

But it wasn't his show, so he'd focus on doing Aunt Roz's version. He'd sat here beside her enough times as a teen to know the drill, often gathering the data from the various sites for her: The Kiro, *built in 1987 in the Yokohama, Japan yards, easily identified by the mismatched patch of blue paint on her starboard bow from her collision with a bridge abutment last fall—fault of a drunken captain, not a broken ship—currently underway from Shanghai with 4,432 TEU of containers of consumer products.*

A TEU was short for a Twenty-foot Equivalent Unit shipping container. As forty-footer lengths were far more standard, it was a good information tidbit to throw in that the ship was actually most likely carrying 2,216 forty-foot containers—which was a mind-boggling amount of "stuff." It was firmly in the Panamax class of ships that could fit through the original Panama Canal locks carrying up to 5,000 TEU. There was a larger class, the Neopanamax class, that could pass through the upgraded Canal locks with 14,000 TEU. Each time one of those loomed over the Columbia Bar, Carlos could only marvel at what was possible.

The Penny, *built...*

Using the MaritimeTraffic.com site, it was easy to see who was inbound and outbound—anyone could who cared. It was the stories behind the ships that kept the podcast so interesting. It's what had originally hooked him. He remembered one poor ship his "Auntie Roz" had reported on that had been pirated four separate times in a single passage. In Indonesia, there'd been a smash-and-grab job clearing out the crew's meager belongings. The second and third—while headed through the South China Sea—they'd had a quarter of their fuel oil siphoned off onto smaller, faster ships in hundred-thousand-gallon thefts. And the fourth pirating off Saipan had actually lasted three days before the pirates had become bored and simply left.

And yet the crews went to sea—a long and lonely life mostly seeking the money to send home to their families who they so rarely saw. Auntie Roz's podcast had given this backbone of international trade a face, at least across the Columbia Bar.

He continued reading down the traffic list.

"That's the shipping that's expected to be *Crossing the Bar* today. Next, in my interview—"

Petty Officer Sarah Goodwin decided that the show host had a good voice, easy to listen to. She and Senior Chief Petty Officer McAllister had been sitting in the Cape D Guard station's communications room, listening to the shipping report and generally slagging each other.

"—we'll be talking to one of the newest of a very rare breed. The USCG Surfmen are the search-and-rescue experts at dozens of US ports."

The Senior Chief had been chapping her ass all morning about Sarah's pending interview on *Crossing the Bar.* That he was the one who'd tagged it onto her duty roster for the day hadn't bothered him. Not even a little. His final instruction to "play nice" with the podcaster they both knew was a complete waste of breath.

Three older brother Coasties and a Coastie mom? Plus her career as a one-out-of-five woman in the service hadn't taught her a thing about "nice." Mom had been through the Guard when she was more like one-in-twenty and had always told Sarah that being twice as hard-ass as any male was the only way to sail.

"And now I'd like to introduce you to the Coast Guard's newest surfwoman—"

She managed to get in the last word on the Senior Chief about playing nice.

"Seriously, Senior Chief?" Then flipped her own microphone live.

"—Petty Officer Sarah Goodwin. Hello, Sarah."

"Hey, Carlos. Thanks for having me on your 'cast," she offered in her sweetest voice while smiling at McAllister. "And it's Surfman. Just because a guy stows extra gear between his legs, doesn't mean he gets the title and I don't. We both had to pass through the same school to earn it."

McAllister rolled his eyes at her. If the man ever slouched, he'd have slouched in the chair in front of the console with utter resignation. Perfect.

She gave him the finger which earned her a smile. Any school with someone like "Mac" McAllister as an instructor made her damn proud to simply have survived, never mind passed.

"Surf*man* Sarah," the podcaster acknowledged without a stumble. Give him a point for that. "Or are you going to be updating the Coast Guard service so that all the guys will be called Surfwomen as well?"

And just that fast she went cold despite the warm office on the temperate September day. Actors versus Actresses. Heroes versus heroines. Waitresses. Stewardesses. That had been the world Mom had fought so hard against. Sarah was so damn sick of it. Her big brothers had been relentless on pushing that button, which had only made her dig in harder. Most of her hand-to-hand combat skills hadn't come from Coast Guard boot camp—they'd come from brawling with her brothers. Now they were scattered across the country by their different posts in the Guard, which was just as well.

McAllister must have seen something in her face, because his look went serious and he tapped his ear to remind her that she was on a live podcast. *Crossing the Bar* had a daily following in the tens of thousands and had always been supportive of the Coast Guard.

She managed to suppress the growl, but not the tone as she replied to Mr. Jerk Carlos Torres. "I'd never expect the men to meet the high standard such a title would require."

"And what would those extra qualifications be, Surf*man* Sarah?" Torres didn't have a clue how close he was to dying on the air. "Must be something pretty amazing. After all, it *is* an amazing list of skills to make Surfman, isn't it?"

It was. She found herself answering him out of habit —so many people didn't know about the training so she'd had lots of practice—explaining just what it took to get here. The familiar litany brought her back from the edge.

Join up, boot camp, Seaman, boat operations…

Somewhere along the way make Petty Officer Third Class. Schools. Choosing your rating.

Boatswain's Mate.

Lots more schools. And a serious amount of time

doing "striker" on-the-job training. One of the proudest days of her life had been achieving her BM1— Boatswain's Mate 1st Class.

"No one outside the 'wet' military really understands what that means. The BM rating means that you have to know everything from winching strength on a cable to a crewman's capabilities, weather, sea, boats—the list goes on. Then you add to that. By becoming a coxswain, it doesn't just mean that you steer the boat. When the weather is busting sixty knots and breaking-wave-hell twenty meters over some poor sucker's head, it's your call on how to save them."

"And you're now passed or certified or whatever to do all that?" She became aware that the interviewer had been coaxing her along, feeding her questions. When had he taken control and she lost it?

McAllister was gone—apparently deciding she wasn't about to disgrace the Guard. Fool.

"Yes. That's what being awarded a Surfman Badge means."

The interviewer gave a low whistle of surprise that almost sounded impressed. "Damn, woman."

And there it was again. There had to be a way that she could whup that out of at least one male's head.

Then she had an idea.

A nasty idea.

It *definitely* wouldn't involve playing nice.

3

C arlos glanced up at the sky and decided that he shouldn't be in too much trouble. September in the Pacific Northwest was changeable in mood, but tended toward the more pleasant. It wasn't until October that the weather really flipped. Today was sixty degrees and maybe fifteen miles-an-hour of wind— thirteenish knots he corrected himself. Sailors always thought in nautical miles for reasons passing understanding.

Then he looked down at the dock again and was less sure. The weather here at the Cape Disappointment Coast Guard station in Ilwaco, Washington on the far bank of the wide Columbia River was blowing up stormy right from the gate.

A Senior Chief Petty Officer McAllister, with the sense of humor of a lead brick, had come to fetch him from security.

"Always glad to have a visit from *Crossing the Bar*," he

grumbled a greeting. "Of course your aunt never went out of her way to antagonize my best new Surfman."

Carlos opened his mouth...

McAllister looked *really* unhappy about something.

...so Carlos closed his mouth again.

He'd thought that he and Surf*man* Sarah Goodwin were just having a little friendly banter for the show. In fact, they'd gone on long enough that he'd had to end the show and just keep recording. He'd briefly muted his own connection to Surfman Sarah to promise the podcast listeners that he'd be continuing the interview in future episodes. He'd gotten enough material to make it a five-part series.

Then at the end of the interview, Petty Officer Sarah Goodwin BM1 had asked if he'd like to go out on a training cruise the next day. He knew that Aunt Roz got out on the cargo ships whenever she could. If he was ever going to be serious about taking over the show, he figured he'd have to do the same. And on his first day she'd offered him the chance to try it out.

Also, as a one-up on his aunt, she'd never gone out on the search-and-rescue surf boats. She'd been out with the bar pilots' transport tugs as they motored out to vessels to guide them back over the bar. She'd also had a local helo pilot who exchanged free sightseeing ads on the show for giving her a quick ride out onto the occasional incoming vessel.

But to get out on the working craft of the US Coast Guard, the 47-foot Motor Lifeboat, better known as the 47-MLB, that was a definite coup. He'd planned on getting major mileage out of that at the next family dinner.

Or so he'd thought as he blithely accepted Surfman Sarah's offer.

Aunt Roz's and Dad's brother had been a US Coast Guard helicopter mechanic for thirty years here by the Columbia—still was. And three of his four daughters had married Coasties. (The fourth, Maggie, a total reprobate and the most fun of the lot, had become a helicopter mechanic for a group of firefighters and married one of the team's civilian helo pilots. Total outcast at family gatherings. He hung with her whenever he could.) But what with all the brothers-in-law's training, he knew how to read a ticked-off Coastie.

And when that Coastie was a Senior Chief Petty Officer, Carlos knew the wind was going to be blowing cold no matter what the weather.

The Senior Chief turned to look at him.

Carlos didn't recall coming to a stop at the head of the pier.

"Go on down, boy. Last boat in the line. You *earned* it." This time the Senior's grimace might have been a mocking smile. He slapped Carlos hard enough on the shoulder that it was a miracle he wasn't catapulted out to sea as some part of a Man Overboard (and don't bother rescuing him) Drill. He and the Senior were the same height, and Carlos liked keeping fit, but he had nothing on the man for raw power.

Turning the slam's momentum into a forward stumble, he headed down the pier. There were five of the boats tied up: two to the left, then three to the right—all parked stern-in along narrow floating docks. Another group of three more were moored on another leg of the long pier. Each crew he passed looked down at him from their boats and then made some snide comment he could never quite hear. But he heard the laughter trailing behind him.

The long path of shame.

It was like the long walk to the principal's office, one he'd worn well over the years. "Directionless." "Inattentive." "Joker." (Prankster actually, but he tried not to correct Dr. Bream too often. Pointing out during his first visit with the man that he'd been named for a fish—but a pretty one, good eating too—hadn't earned him as much good will as you might think.) He'd pulled any number of stunts over the years: reprogramming the school bells to ring at odd times and changing out the recording of the national anthem for morning announcements with *Louie Louie* by the Notre Dame Marching Band—the best version in his humble opinion.

Carlos managed to get As when he cared: English, History, Journalism. Cs when he didn't: just about everything else except track-and-field. No college. He'd wanted to get a little "down and dirty." Which had turned out to be less fun than it sounded over the last five years. He'd done some paid blogging, a little sports writing, local cable TV, made it to the news desk. And got bored out of his gourd.

A local broadcast station—a good local in Seattle— offered him a test at a weekend anchor slot.

We think you've got what it takes. We want you to bring it to our market.

He sat in as a "guest co-anchor" for a pair of evening and late-night news slots.

He'd quit the cable station the next day. But instead of turning his car north for Seattle, he'd turned west and ended up in Aunt Roz's Victorian-tower broadcast studio. Quite how or why that had happened still eluded him.

And high school. It had been a long time since Carlos had thought about that long walk down the echoing concrete hallway between all the sports trophies he'd helped win and all the academic awards that he hadn't.

"Shake it off, dude." Though he kept his voice low as another round of titters followed him along. "Yeah, just keep that up, guys. Who knew that full-grown Coasties 'tittered'? Definitely going into the next podcast." He felt better for that decision.

The last boat down the line didn't have a tittering crew watching him go by. They were busy preparing to go to sea.

A pair of guys in full float gear were checking over their equipment. They were dressed in bright red, head-to-toe float suits with the hoods tugged back. Another guy with a clipboard and a toolbelt was conferring with them.

And up on the open bridge, there was a woman standing there like she was a Greek goddess. At least that was his first impression. The sun, still low to the east, was dazzling behind her. She had her feet planted wide and her arms crossed in front of her. She rolled so easily with the rocking of the boat that it seemed she was the one who stayed still and the rest of the world bobbed and dipped around her center. He couldn't see anything else about her because she also wore one of the bulky float suits. Maybe her hair was made of purest gold, maybe that was just the sun—it was hard to tell.

"Mr. Torres. So glad you could join us." Just like on the radio, Petty Office Sarah Goodwin had a low, warm voice that sounded deceptively friendly. In fact, if not for the Senior Chief's warning, he'd have thought it was. Now he could hear the chill sweeping south from Alaska. Or perhaps the Arctic Ocean. Deep chill. He wasn't just in the deep end of the pool; the bottom had gone missing while he wasn't watching.

The 47-MLB was just that, forty-seven feet of custom-designed purebred Motor Lifeboat. He'd done what research he could last night. It was all aluminum. No air-filled bladders that made the smaller 42-foot Near Shore Lifeboat look like a Zodiac on steroids with rubber-bladder sides. Five feet of length was only the smallest of the differences. The 47-MLB had an open bridge exposed to the weather and an enclosed bridge that stayed watertight even if the boat became fully submerged. There was even a watertight survivor compartment complete with medical gear and a stretcher if they had to do a helicopter evacuation. Twin Detroit diesel engines could practically make the boat fly.

It was forty-seven feet, eighteen tons (incredibly light

for a boat of this size), and over a million dollars of mean, robust, Coast Guard machine.

"Thanks for having me." If she was going to pretend to play it light, so could he.

She watched him for a long moment, then shrugged. "Vicks and Marnham. Get him suited up to get wet. You don't mind getting wet, do you?"

"No, ma'am," seemed the safest answer. But he risked adding, "Though usually I'm more of a track-and-field guy." Because why the hell not?

4

S arah managed to keep the smile off her face until she was turned away. The float crew would get him in a suit while she finished checking over the pre-mission list.

Javits came over with his engineer's sign-off that all of his systems were good to go and she sent him to suit up as well.

Track and field.

He had the shape for it. At first she'd thought it was a swimmer's form, all lean except for legs and shoulders. That how you knew a true rescue swimmer. Most swimmers built up the big shoulders, but the real top guys—like Vicks and Marnham—had thighs of steel as well.

Mr. Torres had surprised her. She'd expected a mouse of a man who never crawled out from his mom's basement except to get his delivery pizza. Six foot of strapping Latino with dark curly hair, olive skin, and a bright smile just didn't fit her mental image. Neither did track-and-field. He was built for it with a top-swimmer's legs filling out his jeans. Though while his shoulders were good, they weren't quite broad enough to be a USCG swimmer.

That's what almost made her laugh in his face. How many times had Senior Chief McAllister lambasted her over these last months about making assumptions?

"Every situation is an unknown. Even if you know it, it's an unknown. Next time you bump up against a log, it's going to be a WWII floating mine with your name carved in the rust. Next time you pull up to help a dismasted sailboat, it's going to be the conning tower of a narco-submarine and they're going to come out guns blazing to take your boat. You gonna give it to them, Goodwin?"

"Never, Senior Chief!" she'd shout from full attention.

And then he'd set her another scenario and she'd walk straight into his next trap.

She rubbed her fingers over her Surfman badge: crossed oars over a life preserver. Only a hundred and sixty active-duty men and women wore these. They were the smallest specialty in the entire Coast Guard and the feeling was still shiny and new. No miscreant radio jockey was going to make her feel one bit less than she was.

Carlos Torres was handsome and fit rather than basement-pizza pale. *Fine.* She'd see just how wet he could take.

"Hi." He'd come up beside her without her even

noticing. That was bad; usually she could feel a seagull even thinking about landing on the aft rail of her boat.

"You ready for this?" She wanted to keep him in his place. His dark eyes were dead-level with her own. She scared off a lot of men with her height, but it didn't seem to bother him. He looked damn good in a float suit.

"Always," he replied with that naive ease of the unsuspecting.

"Sit your ass over there," she aimed a finger at the port-side chair. He was in her world now and there was no listening audience to make her pretend to be nice. "Put on the seat belt. You do not take it off without a direct order from me. And if you touch a single control or lever, I will take your belt off myself and throw you overboard. Are we clear?"

"Yes, ma'am." He shot her a salute that said he'd never served. But it was close enough to right that it meant he'd watched too many war movies or something. Also, his smile just grew bigger as if he knew he was pissing her off and was enjoying himself.

She glanced down at the morning's surf report on her own console and made a bet with herself on just how long he wasn't going to keep wearing that smile.

5

"Cushy," Carlos dropped into the chair. "How hard is the ride on this boat?"

Sarah looked over at him with narrowed eyes. Blue eyes that seemed to see everything and true blonde hair just long enough to make a short ponytail. BM Goodwin might sound like a force of nature, but she looked, oddly, like a fighter. It wasn't that she wasn't beautiful, because…well, *damn*. It was that there was a determined set to her expression that he bet could run over anything in her way: man, rough surf, or Neopanamax container ship. He wondered how many times *she'd* tracked the long path down to the principal's office during her high school years. More than a few.

"Why the surprise?" Carlos enjoyed doing that to her.

"Most civilians think the seat is cushy for its own sake."

"Uh-huh. Where you from?"

"Chicago originally."

"Great Lakes. That's heavy duty," Carlos was impressed.

Sarah looked surprised that he knew that as well. Most people didn't even know the Coast Guard also guarded those inland waters among many others. The Great Lakes boasted sixteen Coast Guard stations between ship and air stations—the entire Mississippi River system only boasted four stations. The storms thrown up on the Great Lakes had actually claimed far more ships than the Columbia Bar. Of course they were also far more expansive. Still, she definitely knew about the wind-water dynamic that so many landlubbers didn't understand.

"I grew up local," he explained. "And while I was never crazy enough to surf this section of the Oregon Coast—which requires a wetsuit and no fear of imminent death—I've been out in the chop when it starts blowing a gale with no warning. Most locals don't even get interested in a storm around here until it crosses fifty knots. And it isn't until it gets up into the eighties that we consider trekking out in our pickups to the headlands and watch the thirty-foot surf rolling in under the horizontal rain. I've never been out in a motor lifeboat, but I'm not dumb enough to think this padding is for comfort."

It earned him a grunt of acknowledgement. Then she turned her attention to casting off lines and getting underway.

He noticed that she didn't snap and bark at the crew for all of her unexpected attitude. They all moved with the calm efficiency of an integrated team. That was part of the reason he'd ended up in track-and-field—he sucked at "team." He could do his part of a relay just fine, by treating it as an individual challenge to outperform not only the other teams, but the other members of his own as well. Sarah's team might have all been cogs of the same wheel they were so smooth.

She worked the heavy aluminum steering wheel with one hand and the pair of red-knobbed throttles with the other as if they were extensions of her body. He also noticed that she too wore her seatbelt, meaning she didn't just make him wear his to keep him out of trouble.

Just how rough a ride *had* he agreed to?

Inspecting his own station, he didn't have a wheel. One arm of the chair had a small lever at the end marked "Port" and "Starboard"—steering adjustments if someone had to work from his seat instead of the one with the wheel. He also had a matching pair of the red throttle levers. Carlos made a special note to not even think about bumping any of them. There were engine-speed and rudder-angle indicators, engine start and stop buttons, and not much else. Mounted between their two positions were radar and radios.

In front of her was another radio and some more electronics, but less than he'd expected. The more he looked, the more he realized that it wasn't about someone tending an amazing machine. A 47-MLB was a simple, seaworthy tool used by a capable woman for going to the rescue.

"Superwoman!" The exclamation was just knocked out of him as the boat slipped out from where the Coast

Guard station lay tucked behind Ruby Island and headed into the throat of the Columbia River.

Sarah glared at him. He had about enough of her silent, feminist-action shit.

"Tough, lady. If the superhero uniform fits, wear it."

I f Carlos Torres was busy picturing her in some skintight superhero outfit, she wasn't going to drown him—she was going to gut him like a salmon.

Assumptions, Goodwin. She could hear McAllister even over the roar of the two Detroit diesels as she took them up on the planing hull to twenty-two knots and headed toward the open ocean.

"What's your problem, Torres?" Sarah shouted over to him.

"My problem?" He wasn't clutching the chair arms like some desperate civilian as they began popping over the two-meter waves washing in from the sea. Instead he sat with his hands folded in his lap as calm as could be. "I got no problems. Sunny day. Out for the morning on a 47-MLB with a beautiful and skilled woman who wants to jettison me overboard every time I pay her a compliment. What's up with that anyway?"

"Nothing's up with that," she clenched her jaw and faced the sea.

Directly starboard lay the tip of the half-mile long North Jetty that ran out from Cape D, Washington. It anchored at the end of Peacock Spit, which had probably claimed more shipwrecks than anywhere else in the world over the last two hundred years. Two miles to port lay the tip of the three-mile long South Jetty stretching out from Clatsop Spit at the very top corner of Oregon. In between lay her job.

She scanned the area as they bounced along the wavetops. Five cruisers under fifty feet, agile enough to be doing pretty much whatever they damn well pleased —which created headaches for everyone, accounting for over twenty percent of Coast Guard rescues every season. A twenty-six-foot daysailer tacking neatly across shipping lanes in a gap between passing ships and not looking to be stupid enough to be headed out to sea over the bar. Two inbound container ships and an outbound bulk carrier all showing their transponders on her radar sweep—meant that three of the sixteen bar pilots were working this morning. Everything appeared in order.

"So, you treat compliments as insults out of some sort of self-defense mechanism. That's interesting."

"I thought you were a journalist not a headshrinker."

"Me? No, I'm neither. Just a directionless bum with a radio show for three weeks while Aunt Roz is on vacation."

"And you're fine with that?"

"Why shouldn't I be?"

Because it makes you even lamer to admit it than being a directionless bum in the first place.

"Personally, I've always found overachieving to be a waste of energy."

"So, what *do* you find worthwhile?" She'd thought to run some shore patrols along the South Jetty, but rejected that. She wanted this Carlos Torres to hurt a little. So instead, she swung wide of the North Jetty and turned northwest for the heavy surf off the Peacock Spit.

Javits must have read her mind, because he came up on the bridge with a pair of safety harnesses. He used one to latch Mr. Bum Torres' suit to a safety ring on the bridge so that he was doubly attached to the boat.

Normally her engineer would be in the seat occupied by Torres. Instead, he harnessed into one of the jump seats directly behind his usual position. Nicer than she'd have been, but then Javits was a nice guy.

Vicks and Marnham would be sitting in the Survivor Compartment, belted in and probably playing a game of Gin Rummy. How had they become blasé about getting out on the water? Every single time she escaped the dock was like the first time she'd gone to a rock concert—some part of her disconnected and danced. She'd always been the perfect student: straight As, head of the volleyball team with her height, and anchor on the swim relay team. And she could count the number of kids she was in touch with from high school on a closed fist.

Why had wanting to be best been such a crime?

It wasn't a crime in the Coast Guard. It had value.

Even Vicks and Marnham, with their ever-so-chill game of Rummy, were actually top flight—they just made a whole point pretending they were too cool to care. They were already top-rated swimmers and she knew they spent most of their off hours preparing for the brutal USCG rescue swimmer course—a 24-week challenge with an eighty percent failure rate. They were so good that even McAllister was giving them better than even odds of making it.

She never fraternized inside the Guard. And she'd yet to find a worthwhile man outside the Guard. Good thing she was used to being alone.

Sarah checked the surf ahead. The bright sun glared off the breaking crests, but added little warmth. Temperatures ran a consistent five to ten degrees lower out on the ocean here, especially when the offshore fog banks were nudging shoreward.

A pair of 47-MLBs were "in it" farther up the line— a new Surfman class getting their "scare them off the boat" ride. First day of class, driven straight into the heaviest surf. There were always a couple that decided they were in over their heads and bailed. Even some heavy-weather-certified coxswains bailed after a day in the Cape D surf.

The trick was, the waves always looked milder than they were. From the east, the Columbia pumped a quarter of a million cubic feet per second into the ocean —the fifth largest river by discharge in North America and thirty-eighth in the world. From the south, a northbound sea current traveled up the coast at a couple kilometers per hour. And from the west, or any direction the Pacific Ocean was in the mood for, sea swells that had been building energy across ten thousand kilometers ran into the other two currents and created utter mayhem just where the ships needed to go. When the tide was outbound and the swells were inbound, like this morning, everything doubled up.

She shared a glance with Javits.

He nodded that everything and everyone was ready —which meant he'd already warned the float guys they were headed into the rough. He included a grimace that said she was pushing it.

When she shrugged a reply that maybe she was, he waved her toward the waves. There was a reason she liked this crew. She knew if she rolled them sideways onto their beam's end, the float guys would simply slap a hand down on their Rummy cards until she righted.

Sarah took the first big wave at a sixty-degree angle, goosing the starboard engine hard as the bow lifted up the face. Ten meters of breaking waves slapped the 47-MLB solidly on the butt, slamming her straight as Sarah shot up over the top.

Half the hull went airborne before they tipped and the nose slammed down on the back of the wave. Just like she'd planned.

She heard Torres grunt with the impact as she was judging the next wave. Her obvious move would take her closer to the two boats giving the First Day cruise, which the instructors wouldn't appreciate. Instead, she let the next wave break hard across the deck.

"Take a breath," she shouted to Torres moments before it hit. Which, like walking into one of McAllister's traps, left her with no air of her own while the 47-MLB lay on its side and a couple tons of sea spray robbed them of air. She was the one sputtering by the time they hit clear air.

She cranked the wheel hard and took the next wave —a chaotic slasher from the south—head-on with a burst of diesel power.

Unlike the older 42-MLB that plowed through the waves, the 47 climbed like the champion it was and shot over the top with almost no water on the deck.

All three of them grunted in unison as the bow slammed down and she began carving for the next wave. She needed to check if Torres had hit his limit yet. Scaring a civilian was one thing, terrifying a radio personality was something McAllister wouldn't appreciate. But the last wave had tossed her toward the First Dayers again and she had to concentrate on hitting the next wave at the same angle they did so that all three boats kept their spacing along the wave face.

"Is this pretty typical?" Torres shouted out to her. He didn't sound upset. Instead he was curious.

"Pretty mild for Peacock Point," she shouted back, too busy to say more as she watched Chief Wester on the next boat to see what his next line of attack would be.

"This is about half of what the boat is rated to take," Javits answered for her. He was the boat's mechanic and always thought of everything from that angle. "Of course to us—"

They all held their breaths as a wall of spray slashed over them and she was able to angle away from the other two boats.

"—as passengers, when we're getting up into the

kind of violence this boat can still handle, it will feel about ten times worse."

This time she could feel Torres watching her.

She took advantage of a bad break to the south, to let the next wave slam Torres from behind without warning.

His sputters when they resurfaced were very gratifying.

7

C arlos would have laughed if he had any air. Surfman Sarah Goodwin was definitely out to get him. He'd have to watch himself around her.

He tried to imagine "ten times worse" and decided that he was glad it wouldn't be him feeling it. He'd already bottomed out the chair's heavy padding twice with breath-stealing butt plants. At first he'd felt insulted at Javits doubling Carlos' harness; now he was grateful. It was very comforting to feel firmly attached to the boat when the waves tossed eighteen tons of aluminum and five humans about like a bath toy.

He tried to watch what Sarah was looking for as she surveyed the next wave and drove them into it, but she was too distracting. Her focus, her whole being, had such a clear purpose. Her, the boat, the wave. Tweak a throttle, cock the wheel, brace for the blow, already turning for the next while the boat still shuddered from the hit. Scan right and left. Other waves? Other craft?

No chance to ask as they plunged back into the

roiling mess that was the sea. Waves seemed to come from every direction, yet still she took them one after another. One moment he had a high view out to sea and back to the beach. The next they plunged into a trough where the entire vista was made up of a bowl of wind-shredded water.

After twenty crestings, or maybe twice that, he decided that the two other boats had left when he wasn't paying attention to them. And still Sarah took on the waves.

He wondered if she was even aware of the passage of time.

Not Superwoman, he decided. More like some daughter of Poseidon, Greek God of the Sea.

Maybe she was—

"Help! Somebody help us!" Squawked over the radio in a shrill scream that broke up even as they transmitted. "Please! Can any…hear…? Help!"

"My hands are a little full," Sarah shouted above the roar of the surf and engines, somehow calmly, and nodded toward the two microphones hanging from the center console. "Take the left one and don't say a single word I don't tell you."

He grabbed it, and forgot to hold his breath as the next wave slammed over them. He surfaced coughing seawater out of his lungs.

"Real smooth, Torres."

He nearly strangled himself suppressing the next choking hack.

"Okay, start: This is the US Coast Guard. Please identify."

Carlos held the key to transmit and echoed her words.

"Oh thank God. This is Tom. No one's been answering!"

He shared a smile with Sarah. Damn but the woman had an amazing smile. Made him wonder just how rarely she let it out to play. It shifted her from stern to whimsical in a single flash of brightness.

"Hi, Tom," he echoed Sarah as she drove hard to the south back toward the main mouth of the river. The waves were so rough, he couldn't sight land, but the sun was to the south and it was blinding him at the moment. "What's the problem and where are you?"

"We were trying. To enter the Columbia. Got swept past it. Big waves! Like nothing I've ever seen! Now they're worse— Shit!"

The last word was Carlos' own.

He shot out an arm as Sarah scowled at him. Just off the starboard side of the 47-MLB, the prow of a sailboat shot out of a wave—not over the top, but straight out of the center of a towering wave face.

It was aimed straight for the back of Sarah's head.

He grabbed her shoulder and hauled her down until her head was practically in his lap. It would have been if her seatbelt hadn't been pulled so tight.

The white V of fiberglass crunched into the stout railing close by her right arm. It slid back along the rail, slamming into one of the uprights supporting the radar mast, then the prow fell astern. The boat rolled in the waves. Tumbling sideways, he briefly saw the keel as it rolled completely over.

Sarah was sitting up and he tried to give a helpful shove.

Her hands were slamming the controls even as she moved.

"Deep breath!" She shouted. "We'll right in twelve seconds."

Carlos gasped in deeply and wondered what she meant, just as he felt the next roller slam into him from behind. The sailboat had knocked them beam-on to the biggest wave he'd seen yet.

All sense of direction disappeared. Gravity was doing one thing. His float suit was doing another with its buoyancy. And his gut was doing a third as the seatbelt yanked him along with the boat's roll.

The pressure built as the water did its best to rip him bodily out of his seat.

This wasn't spray.

He was completely submerged in "green" water— the solid wall of true ocean.

Blinking against the saltwater made it feel as if his eyeballs were being ripped from his head. The pressure built against his eardrums.

Sarah had shouted something other than to take a breath.

Twelve seconds.

It had already been minutes. He could feel the pressure squeezing his chest, telling him to breathe. He wanted to claw at his seatbelt to free himself, but remembered the second harness. No idea how it had attached.

By an act of pure will, he began counting backwards

from twelve and picturing the long hall of the school's meaningless trophy display.

Twelve, the debate club.

Eleven, the math team on the right.

These were going to be the last images of his life?

Ten, basketball on the left.

Really? Pathetic!

Nine, the cheer squad of all ridiculous things (the school's only state-level competitor other than his own track-and-field All-State that year).

He needed to get a different life next time.

Eight, the yearbook club.

Like that was something he cared about.

Seven, *The Feed*, the online school news forum he'd run for two years had won a statewide broadcasting award.

Six—

He slammed back into the air as the boat completed its roll, tipping far enough over the other way that he gasped in a fresh breath in prep for going under again. They mostly righted so he didn't need it.

"Still with us, Tom?" Somehow he'd held onto the microphone and managed to echo Sarah's words.

The silence was ominous as he scanned around looking for the sailboat. They didn't always right themselves the way the MLB was designed to.

"There," Sarah was already turning for it as another wave tumbled it upright. No mast. That's why Tom hadn't been able to reach anyone. Losing his mast, he'd lost his antenna. The only reason they'd heard him was they were so close they were getting the bleed directly off his transmitter.

Glancing back, Carlos saw that somehow the two members of the float team had managed to get onto the rear deck and were moving confidently along it. He noted they each had a safety harness with two clips, one of which was always attached somewhere on the boat.

He tried Tom again, with no luck.

He twisted to look at Javits in the seat behind his, to see if he needed Carlos to do something. No Javits.

Before Carlos could panic, he spotted him on the afterdeck. Somehow he'd negotiated down a five-step ladder while they were being tumbled about. Even as Carlos watched, Javits began pulling two-inch yellow polypropylene line off one of the two big drums mounted there.

In moments, Vicks was in the water. Marnham was paying out a line attached to Vick's harness as the man swam toward the leaping sailboat while dragging the two-inch line with him.

Somehow, in the impossible surf, Sarah had gotten them lined up stern-first in front of the sailboat. Each time a wave battered them, the swimmer resurfaced somewhere closer to the sailboat.

The next time the sailboat's bow dug into the face of a wave, Vicks rode the wave crest above it—his arms moving like pinwheels in a hurricane. Then he was lifted out of the water as the bow emerged sluggishly from beneath him. In moments, he had the yellow line tied off on the bow's anchor cleat. Then he began moving aft.

"Tom?" Carlos tried the radio again as Sarah added power to the engines.

"…insid… Think we capsiz…"

"Tom. Listen, there is a Coast Guard swimmer on your boat. Move to the rear, but do not try to exit the cabin until he reaches you."

"O..ay."

A wave swept the sailboat end to end. Vicks rode it like a surfer down the length of the deck, then managed to catch himself on a lifeline stanchion before he was swept overboard.

"That boat isn't long for the world," he shouted at Sarah. It was wallowing lower with each inundation.

8

Regrettably Carlos' assessment matched hers.
She'd hoped to drag them out into calmer water, then remembered the forecast. Surf building through the morning. There'd been a storm somewhere out at sea and the ocean swell had kept moving even without the storm pushing at it any longer.

The rougher water had been teaching her its own lessons this morning. It was a rare opportunity to learn and she'd concentrated on studying the interplay of the truly big surf. McAllister had told her stories of what waves could do—and her long stretch at the National Motor Lifeboat School had taught her a lot. But today had been running rougher even than usual for Peacock Spit, so now she had the images and the body memory to attach to McAllister's tales.

Until the sailboat tried to kill her.

Capsized, dismasted, she still should have seen it.

Somehow.

Carlos had. When it counted, he'd kept his head as

well as any Guardsman and that was an unexpected gift. He'd also saved her at least a bad battering.

A quick glance showed that tops of the waves were tearing off spindrifts of spray. No longer merely rough surf—the wind had blown up a fresh gale of forty knots while she'd been working the boat. She grabbed the other mic that would connect her to the Coast Guard station.

"This is MLB 562 in tow with a dismasted Cal 39 sailboat three miles due west of Peacock Spit. Forecast?"

"Blowing forty, climbing to fifty over the next hour. Seas your location twelve meters, expecting fast build to fifteen-plus. Do you require assistance?"

"Swimmer on a line aboard the Cal 39. Effecting rescue of one crew…"

Carlos flashed two fingers, then waggled the hand in doubt as he raised a third.

She thought about it. Tom *had* kept referring to "we."

Sarah spun the wheel to take the next wave on the starboard quarter.

"…possibly two or more. Helo aloft in case we need eyes. Cal 39 will be gone under before second MLB could arrive. Out." She hung up the microphone.

"What's my status, Carlos?" She couldn't afford to look away from the waves. The MLB could function effectively to sixty knots of wind and twenty-meter waves, but doing a rescue in those conditions was right out at the limits.

"You've got about fifty feet of tow line to the Cal

which has barely a foot of freeboard now. Vicks has gone into the cabin which must be mostly flooded."

She calculated the time to haul two civilians across the gap separating the boats as she ducked under a major breaker that actually slapped the MLB's bow under the water rather than letting it ride over. Getting under the curl of a breaking wave was always a bad idea.

But her baby rode it out—splitting the wave across the front of the bridge and only hitting them with spray. The MLB finally popped up like a cork with enough force to nearly cut Sarah in two with her seatbelt. They were all going to be black-and-blue after this one.

Carlos blew out a loud breath beside her, then glanced back.

"No boat. No boat. No boat... There! On the surface, awash."

Out of options, Sarah cut the power to both engines.

Then she turned and saw that the situation was just as bad as she imagined.

Drifting backwards, she used a small burst of starboard power to avoid ramming the sailboat's bow with her stern.

Javits was winding the line back onto the drum as fast as he could, but the drum was built for strength not speed.

"Prepare to cut," she shouted as loudly as she could. They were less than ten feet apart, but the roar of wind and water—she could only hope that he heard her.

They pulled parallel with the bow.

"Cut!" she yelled and continued drifting back. The

47-MLB had a walkway along either side of the cabin. It ran from the aft deck to the foredeck, five feet above the water. But by flipping up a grating, a notch in the hull formed a recovery well that was just a foot above the water.

The others would know what she was doing.

She hoped.

Pulling alongside any craft in such rough seas was incredibly dangerous. Shifting across two or more injured civilians and a CG swimmer was a wild gamble at best, but she didn't have another play. If she ordered them all into the water, could the approaching helo even find them again in such turbulent wave conditions? Not likely. Not until they were corpses washed up on the vast sandy stretches of Long Beach to the north.

The training that had been driven straight into her instincts kept her concentrated on her part of the mission—looking down over the starboard side of her boat and trying to calculate how to keep it within a foot of the sinking sailboat as the waves slammed them about. The wind was from the port side—trying to topple her over on top of the sailboat—and it wasn't as if she had a bow thruster to hold herself in place sideways.

But the MLB would offer some wind and wave shield for the rescue, so she'd taken the upwind side. Which should work.

Hopefully.

She could feel Torres straining to see what was happening over her side of the boat.

"Do *not* unharness from your seat," she shouted at

him. "Keep watch to port and let me know if anything big is coming."

"Define big," he answered on a half-laugh, commenting on the biggest surf she'd certainly ever driven in. His laugh cut off in a choke as spray inundated them for a moment.

9

Sarah wasn't sure how she'd let herself get talked into this, but there was no backing out.

You owe me at least a beer for trying to kill me, Carlos had said at the dock as the ambulance took away Tom and his girlfriend (two broken wrists and a concussion between them).

In a fit of weakness, she'd agreed. She should have known he'd turn it into a beer and a pizza, which was far too much like a date.

Inferno Lounge.

Perfect, she was in hell.

Carlos had beat her there, because—of all stupid things—she'd vacillated on what to wear. Like her wardrobe held so many options. Jeans, a blouse, and a fleece vest, because Oregon evenings were always cool by definition. Then she'd had to double back for a windbreaker, because it was September. Then for her wallet because she was a basket case.

It would have been easy if it had just been dinner

with Carlos Torres from *Crossing the Bar.* He'd done a damned decent job of being an asset instead of a liability on the rescue.

It was much more complicated after she'd listened to his latest couple of podcasts. He'd interlaced her initial interview with his own observations about the Surfman training and then the rescue. It had been…riveting.

"Damn. You're hired, Goodwin." Senior Chief McAllister told her after they'd listened to it together.

"Didn't do anything unusual, Senior Chief."

"Not for you, maybe. Your request of station assignment better be on my desk in the morning and it better say Cape Disappointment in all three preference slots or you and I are going to have words, Missy. Search-and-rescue for now. Assistant Instructor as soon as a slot opens." Then he'd stomped off.

She'd *Missy* him a good one next chance she had.

But now she had to deal with the man who had just gotten the Coast Guard's National Motor Lifeboat School an international recognition. Carlos' story had been picked up by the major news feeds. The only way she'd protected herself was by declaring he had an exclusive on the story and routing all of the reporters' calls to *Crossing the Bar's* phone number.

"Hey Surf*woman*," Carlos rose to his feet as she approached the table.

"And the reason I'm not killing you for that?"

He smiled broadly, "Because you already proved my point."

"Which is?"

"You proved that Surf*woman* is indeed a superior standard that mere Surf*men* can only hope to live up to."

Sarah sighed and dropped into a seat across from him. The Inferno Lounge wasn't as hideous as the name. It was a comfortable old bar and restaurant out on the edge of the waterfront. Rather than taking a table in some dark corner, Carlos had chosen one up against the big sweep of glass. Just feet away lay the broad reach of the Columbia. The bridge between Astoria, Oregon and Ilwaco, Washington, arched against the deep orange and gold of the sunset sky. From here she could see all of the shipping moving through the mouth of the Columbia. He'd even sat so that her seat looked out to sea while his looked upriver, which was decent of him—she knew him well enough now to know that the thoughtfulness was intentional.

"You asked me a question," he said after they'd ordered beer and a loaded pizza.

"I…when? What was it?"

"You asked what I was, a headshrinker or a journalist? And I told you that I was just a directionless bum. You asked if I was okay with that."

"You said you were."

"I lied."

"Still doesn't tell me if you were a journalist or a headshrinker."

Carlos smiled at her. It was a strange smile. More as if he was smiling at himself.

"What?"

"You really want to know the answer?"

She shrugged a yes.

"My problem was," and he aimed those dark eyes of his at her. She suddenly couldn't look away. "That in that moment, I had just figured out that you and I graduated from school the same year. Made me feel like I hadn't don't shit with my life. Hell of a depressing thought for a sunny day out on the ocean."

"No, you've——" He rested a warm hand on hers for a moment and silenced her.

"I said *was.*"

"Oh no. You're one of those Word People, aren't you?" Sarah couldn't suppress a groan. Her middle brother was that way, stopping the most normal conversation to clarify, rectify, prevaricate——whatever. "Words always have meaning and you have to use just the right one?"

"Guilty as charged. Professional journalist, amateur headshrinker."

Maybe she could like him despite that. Maybe not. She'd wait and see.

"Just a week before I met you, I got the golden job call. *Come be a news anchor at a major station.* It was weekend anchor, but it was a good slot. Real opportunity."

"But you're here."

"Yep," he sipped his beer after it arrived and looked out at a passing bulk carrier headed to Portland to onload soda ash. "And I didn't know why either. I'd gotten in the car headed to Seattle——and ended up in my aunt's driveway here in Astoria."

"You know why now?" She tasted her own beer, a local porter she hadn't known——not much reason to go get a pint when you weren't seeing anyone.

"I do." And he didn't explain.

"And?" Guessing games weren't her strength either.

He just pointed at her.

"What? You're suddenly in love with me?"

"No, that'll come later."

She opened her mouth, then closed it again so that she didn't choke on some random wave that might crash over her unexpectedly.

"You'll have to meet the family first. We're quite a local clan here. A lot of Coasties, a few firefighters," then he tapped himself on the chest, "and the new broadcaster of *Crossing the Bar*. Survive one of those family dinners, then we'll talk over the falling in love part."

Meeting his family? No way in hell was she meeting any lame-ass bum's— Except Carlos wasn't. Or was he? She didn't know what to think.

"I don't do what you do. But I realized that I do know how to tell others about that."

He certainly did. She was still breathless from hearing his recounting of the rescue, which had covered a mere twelve lines in her official report. That he saw her the way he did. Powerful and female. Competent, worthy, and desirable. All mixed together. All in one person she barely recognized.

Her mother had always delineated that you could either be a woman or a member of the military and that doing both wasn't possible. Not on the outside. And Sarah had taken that into the inside as well until she'd totally believed it.

Carlos was showing her that perhaps that wasn't true.

"And," Carlos continued. This time she could feel that his smile was for her. "I'm especially good if it's something I care about. I was raised here. My family is here. Cousins, sisters, uncles, parents, Aunt Roz, all of them. Thanks to you, I know that I came back here rather than going to Seattle because I care about *this* place. I care about *these* people." He waved a hand at the shipping channel so nearby, now shadowed in the evening light.

It was a breathtaking statement. Sarah's family was…scattered. Rarely coming together because they were a Coastie family and one person's leave never matched another's. Not that they'd ever been that close to begin with.

Carlos had an anchor. No, he *was* an anchor. It wasn't the sort of thing to merely respect—it was something to admire. She could feel the strength of it, the holding power of that inner anchor so firmly set within him.

"Best part," he leaned back and paused while the pizza was delivered and they each had burned their mouths on the first searing bite.

"Is?" Sarah prompted him.

"Found a woman that I know I'm going to care about just as much as all the rest of them. Even more, if that's possible."

Sarah took another bite and decided that Carlos was probably right about that, too.

Didn't mean she was going to make it easy for him. But…yeah, he was right.

If you liked this, you'll love:
Fire Light, Fire Bright.
And we love getting reviews, too!

FIRE LIGHT, FIRE BRIGHT (EXCERPT)

A WILDFIRE HOTSHOTS ROMANCE

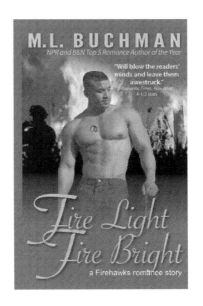

EXCERPT OF FIRE LIGHT, FIRE BRIGHT

"Hi, I'm Candace Cantrell. First Rule: anyone who calls me Candy, who isn't my dad," she hooked a thumb at Fire Chief Carl Cantrell standing at-ease beside her, "is gonna get my boot up their ass. We clear on that?"

A rolling mumble of "Yes, ma'am." "Clear." and "Got it, Candace." rippled back to her from the recruits. Some answered almost as softly as the breeze working its way up through the tall pines. Others trumpeting it out as if to get her notice. A few offered simple nods.

She surveyed the line of recruits slowly. Way too early to make any judgments, but it was tempting. Day One, Minute One, and she could already guess five of the forty applicants weren't going to make it into the twenty slots she had open.

The one thing they all, including her dad, needed to see right up front was their team leader's complete confidence. Candace had been fighting wildfires for the U.S. Forest Service hotshot teams for a decade. She'd worked her way up to foreman twice, and had been gunning for a shot at superintendent of a whole twenty-person crew when her dad had called.

"We're got permission to form up an IHC in the heart of the Okanagan-Wenatchee National Forest," he never was long on greetings over the phone.

Her mouth had watered. A brand new Interagency Hotshot Crew didn't happen all that often.

"I talked to the other captains and we want you to form it up."

Now her throat had gone dry and she had to fight to not let it squeak.

"Me?"

"You aren't gonna let me down now, Candy Girl?"

"You shittin' me?" Not a chance.

Then he'd hit her with that big belly laugh of his.

"Knew you'd like the idea."

And simple as that, she'd been out of the San Juan IHC at the end of the Colorado fire season and back home in the Cascade Mountains of Washington State. She'd grown up in the resort town of Leavenworth— two thousand people and a ka-jillion tourists. The city fathers had transformed the failing timber town into a Bavarian wonderland back in the sixties. But that didn't stop the millions of acres of the National Forest and the rugged sagebrush-steppe ecosystem further east in central Washington from torching off every summer.

The very first thing she'd done, before she'd even left the San Juan IHC, was to call in a pair of ringers as her two foremen. Jess was short, feisty, and could walk up forested mountains all day with heavy gear without slowing down a bit. Patsy was tall, quiet, and tough. Candace had them stand in with the crews for the first days because she wanted their eyes out there as well.

"Second, see that road?" she asked the recruits and pointed to the foot of National Forest Road 6500. She'd had their first meet-up be here rather than at the fire hall in town. A gaggle of vehicles were pulled off the dirt of Little Wenatchee River Road. Beater pickups dominated, but there were a couple of hammered Civics, a pair of muscle cars, and a gorgeous Harley Davidson that she considered stealing it was so sweet.

The recruits all looked over their shoulders at the one lane of dirt.

"We're going for a stroll up that road. We leave in sixty seconds."

Like a herd of sheep, they all swung their heads to look at her.

"Fifty-five seconds, and this ain't gonna be a Sunday stroll."

You could tell the number of seasons they'd fought fire just by their reactions.

Five or more? They already wore their boots. Daypacks with water and energy bars were kept on their shoulders during her intro. And despite it being Day One of the ten-day shakedown, all had some tools: fold-up shovel and a heavy knife strapped to their leg at a minimum. Only she, Jess, and Patsy had Pulaski wildland fire axes tied to their gear, but all the veterans knew the drill.

Three to four seasons? Groans and eyerolls. Packs were on the ground beside them. No tools, but they knew what was coming now that she'd told them—ten kilometers, at least, and not one meter of it flat.

One to two seasons? Had the right boots on, but no packs. They were racing back to their vehicles to see what equipment they could assemble.

Rookies? Tennis shoes, ball caps, no gear, blank stares.

"Forty-five seconds, rooks. Boots and water. If you're not on the trail in fifty seconds, you're off the crew." That got their asses moving.

There was one man on the whole crew she couldn't pigeonhole, the big guy who'd climbed off the Harley. His pack and the fold-up shovel strapped to it were so new they sparkled. But his boots and the massive hunting knife on his thigh both showed very heavy use.

A glance at her Dad's assessing gaze confirmed it. Something was odd about the Harley man and his easy grin. Not rugged handsome, but still very nice to look at. Powerful shoulders, slim waist. Not an athlete's build, but rather someone who really used his body. His worn jeans revealed that he already had the powerful legs that every hotshot would develop from endless miles of chasing fire over these mountains and steppes for the next six months. It was like he was a Hollywood movie: some parts of him were so very right, but a lot of the details were dead wrong.

Click here to keep reading at fine retailers everywhere.

ABOUT THE AUTHOR

M.L. Buchman started the first of over 50 novels and even more short stories while flying from South Korea to ride across the Australian Outback. All part of a solo around-the-world bicycle trip (a mid-life crisis on wheels) that ultimately launched his writing career.

Booklist has selected his military and firefighter series(es) as 3-time "Top 10 Romance of the Year." NPR and Barnes & Noble have named other titles "Top 5 Romance of the Year." In 2016 he was a finalist for RWA's RITA award.

He has flown and jumped out of airplanes, can single-hand a fifty-foot sailboat, and has designed and built two houses. In between writing, he also quilts. M.L. is constantly amazed at what can be done with a degree in geophysics. He also writes: contemporary romance, thrillers, and SF. More info at: www.mlbuchman.com

Join the conversation:
www.mlbuchman.com

Other works by M. L. Buchman:

SIGN UP FOR M. L. BUCHMAN'S NEWSLETTER TODAY

and receive:
Release News
Free Short Stories
a Free book

Do it today. Do it now.
http://free-book.mlbuchman.com

or
Subscribe to get every story a week early, and cheaper!
http://www.patreon.com/mlbuchman

Printed in Great Britain
by Amazon